Dear Parents:

Congratulations! Your child is taking the first steps on an exciting journey. The destination? Independent reading!

STEP INTO READING® will help your child get there. The program offers five steps to reading success. Each step includes fun stories and colorful art or photographs. In addition to original fiction and books with favorite characters, there are Step into Reading Non-Fiction Readers, Phonics Readers and Boxed Sets, Sticker Readers, and Comic Readers—a complete literacy program with something to interest every child.

Learning to Read, Step by Step!

Ready to Read Preschool–Kindergarten
• big type and easy words • rhyme and rhythm • picture clues
For children who know the alphabet and are eager to begin reading.

Reading with Help Preschool–Grade 1
• basic vocabulary • short sentences • simple stories
For children who recognize familiar words and sound out new words with help.

Reading on Your Own Grades 1–3
• engaging characters • easy-to-follow plots • popular topics
For children who are ready to read on their own.

Reading Paragraphs Grades 2–3
• challenging vocabulary • short paragraphs • exciting stories
For newly independent readers who read simple sentences with confidence.

Ready for Chapters Grades 2–4
• chapters • longer paragraphs • full-color art
For children who want to take the plunge into chapter books but still like colorful pictures.

STEP INTO READING® is designed to give every child a successful reading experience. The grade levels are only guides; children will progress through the steps at their own speed, developing confidence in their reading.

Remember, a lifetime love of reading starts with a single step!

Thomas the Tank Engine & Friends™

CREATED BY BRITT ALLCROFT

Based on The Railway Series by The Reverend W Awdry.
© 2014 Gullane (Thomas) LLC.
Thomas the Tank Engine & Friends and Thomas & Friends are trademarks of Gullane (Thomas) Limited.
HIT and the HIT Entertainment logo are trademarks of HIT Entertainment Limited.
All rights reserved. Published in the United States by Random House Children's Books, a division of Random House LLC, 1745 Broadway, New York, NY 10019, and in Canada by Random House of Canada Limited, Toronto, Penguin Random House Companies.

Step into Reading, Random House, and the Random House colophon are registered trademarks of Random House LLC.

Visit us on the Web!
StepIntoReading.com
randomhouse.com/kids
www.thomasandfriends.com

Educators and librarians, for a variety of teaching tools, visit us at RHTeachersLibrarians.com

ISBN 978-0-385-37388-3 (trade) — ISBN 978-0-375-97323-9 (lib. bdg.) — ISBN 978-0-375-98213-2 (ebook)

Printed in the United States of America
10 9 8 7 6 5 4 3 2 1

HiT entertainment

THOMAS & FRIENDS™

THE MONSTER OF SODOR

Based on The Railway Series
by The Reverend W Awdry

Illustrated by Richard Courtney

Random House 🏠 New York

It is a sunny day
on the Island of Sodor.

Thomas is working
in the clay pits.

Thomas sees
giant footprints
in the rock.

6

The footprints
are scary!

What made them?

Thomas tells Percy
what he saw.

Percy thinks a monster
made the prints!
He is scared.

The next day
Percy goes
back to work.

He sees a dark shadow
up ahead!

Is it a monster?

No!

It is a new engine
named Gator.

Percy and Gator
are friends now.
But Percy is still
scared of monsters!

Gator tells Percy
to be brave
even if he is scared.

A big ship
is leaving Sodor.

Percy wants to go, too.

Gator says
running away
is not very brave.

Thomas wants
Percy to stay.
He sees the ship!

Pull, Cranky, pull!

The boat stops

just in time.

CRANKY

But Percy is not

on the boat!

He has gone back
to the clay pits.
He wants to see
the footprints.

Percy chuffs
up the mountain.
The ground shakes.
Rocks fall down.

Something big

falls near Percy.

He is sure
it is a monster!

But it is not a monster.

It is a dinosaur fossil!

Percy has made
a Really Useful
discovery!

The footprints were
made a long time ago.

Percy solved

the monster mystery!